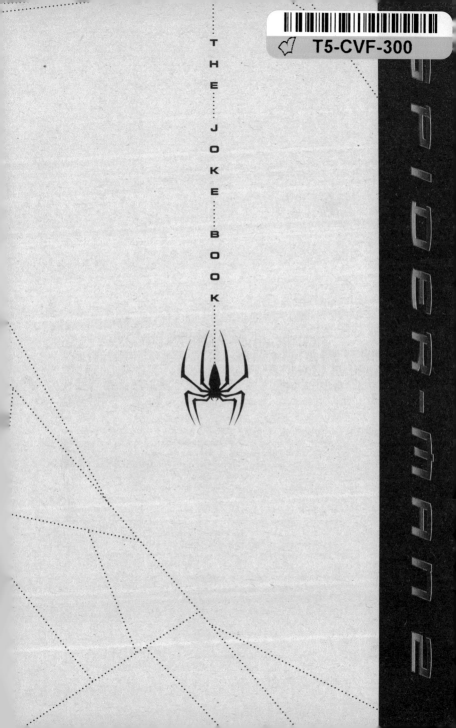

THE JOKE BOOK

SPIDER-MAN 2

T5-CVF-300

COLUMBIA PICTURES PRESENTS A MARVEL ENTERPRISES/LAURA ZISKIN PRODUCTION
TOBEY MAGUIRE "SPIDER-MAN" 2" KIRSTEN DUNST JAMES FRANCO ALFRED MOLINA ROSEMARY HARRIS DONNA MURPHY
MUSIC BY DANNY ELFMAN EXECUTIVE PRODUCERS STAN LEE KEVIN FEIGE EXECUTIVE PRODUCER JOSEPH M. CARACCIOLO BASED ON THE MARVEL COMIC BOOK BY STAN LEE AND STEVE DITKO
SCREEN STORY BY DAVID KOEPP AND ALFRED GOUGH & MILES MILLAR SCREENPLAY BY ALVIN SARGENT PRODUCED BY LAURA ZISKIN AVI ARAD DIRECTED BY SAM RAIMI

MARVEL   SPIDER-MAN CHARACTER ® & © 2004 MARVEL CHARACTERS, INC. ALL RIGHTS RESERVED.   sony.com/Spider-Man   COLUMBIA PICTURES

Spider-Man 2™: The Joke Book

For information address HarperCollins Children's Books,
a division of HarperCollins Publishers,
1350 Avenue of the Americas, New York, NY 10019.
Library of Congress catalog card number: 2003111610
Typography by: Joe Merkel
1 2 3 4 5 6 7 8 9 10
❖
First Edition

www.harperchildrens.com
www.sony.com/Spider-Man

SPIDER-MAN 2™
THE JOKE BOOK

By Thea Feldman
Based on the Motion Picture
Screenplay by Alvin Sargent
Screen Story by David Koepp
and Alfred Gough & Miles Millar
Based on the Marvel Comic Book
by Stan Lee and Steve Ditko

HarperFestival®
A Division of HarperCollinsPublishers

IT SEEMED LIKE A BRIGHT IDEA

How did Dr. Otto Octavius present his new project?

Energetically.

What was the subject of Dr. Octavius's presentation?

Current events.

What did Peter think of Dr. Octavius's experiment?

It was enlightening.

What did Peter say when he heard about Dr. Octavius's fusion ideas?

"More power to you!"

How did the audience feel about Dr. Octavius's experiment?

They had to admit it had a certain flare.

How would you describe Doc Ock?

At times, he was re-volting.

What did the Tritium do?

It fueled Doc Ock's passion.

Why did Dr. Octavius put on the smart-arms harness?

He wanted to do hands-on work.

How did Dr. Octavius really feel about putting on the harness?
It needled him.

What happened when Dr. Octavius put on the harness?
He went on Otto-pilot.

Could Dr. Octavius drive after the experiment went wrong?
No, his motor function was impaired.

Was Dr. Octavius out of line when he wouldn't stop the experiment?
Well, he did over-react.

SURFING THE WEB

What kind of hero did Spider-Man often think he was?
Full of baloney.

How did Spider-Man feel about saving people?
It put a little spring in his step.

What do you get when you cross Peter with...

...a botanical garden?
A spider-plant.

...a book of etiquette?
Spider-Manners.

...a potato?
Spudder-Man.

...a banana?
A spider-monkey.

What do you get when you mix Spider-Man with corn?

A cob-web.

What do you call Peter when he hasn't combed his hair?

Spider-Mangy.

*If there were several webbed avengers,
what would you call them?*
Spider-Many.

Where does Peter like to live?
Spider-Manhattan.

*Where does Peter keep a picture of Aunt
May?*
On the Spider-Mantel.

If Peter became rich, where would he live?
In a Spider-Mansion.

What kind of web does Spider-Man use when he wants to chat with his friends?
An Inter-net.

What do you call it when you see Spider-Man swinging from one building to another?
A Web-sight.

Why would J. J. Jameson not make a good Spider-Man?
Because he always spins things the wrong way.

How does Spider-Man feel when he's tense?
Strung out.

How can you tell that Peter is good with computers?
He is a web-master.

Where does Spider-Man go when he's at a loss for words?
Web-ster's Dictionary.

What is Spider-Man's favorite season?
Spring.

What is Spider-Man's least favorite season?
Fall.

What is Spider-Man's favorite day of the week?
Webs-day.

What is Spider-Man's favorite month?
Web-ruary.

What is Spider-Man's favorite kind of music?
Swing.

What is Doc Ock's favorite day?
Sun-day.

What is Doc Ock's favorite month?

Ock-tober.

Why did Peter move to the city?

He wanted to be a Central
Parker.

SOME TOUGH KNOCKS

Knock, knock.

Who's there?

Ock.

Ock who?

Ock-asionally my experiments work.

Knock, knock.

Who's there?

Pizza.

Pizza who?

Pizza Parker, just like his Uncle Ben.

Knock, knock.

Who's there?

Arms.

Arms who?

Arms so glad you opened the door.

SPIDER-MAN 2

Knock, knock.

Who's there?

Osborn.

Osborn who?

Osborn in New York City, what about you?

Knock, knock.

Who's there?

Harry.

Harry who?

Harry spider bit Peter and turned him into Spider-Man!

Knock, knock.

Who's there?

Aunt May.

Aunt May who?

**Aunt May carry off the picnic
if you're not careful!**

Knock, knock.

Who's there?

Sun.

Sun who?

**Sun-thing tells me the fusion reaction
isn't working right!**

Knock, knock.

Who's there?

Otto.

Otto who?

Otto know not to play with atomic power!

HEARTBEAT

Why did the astronaut fall in love with M. J.?
She had star quality.

How did the astronaut feel about M. J.?
He was over the moon about her.

What did M. J. think of the astronaut?
She thinks he's out of this world.

What did Peter think of John?

He wished the guy were an astro-*naught*.

Did M. J. mean to fall in love with an astronaut?

No, she didn't plan-et.

If Spider-Man and M. J. wanted to get married, what would they plan?

A huge webbing!

IT'S ALL IN THE TIMING

What would you call John if he swallowed his watch on the moon?

A luna-tick.

Why did Peter check the clock tower?

Because it was high time.

What was Peter when he landed on the clock tower?

On time—for once.

Knock, knock.

Who's there?

Eight o'clock.

Eight o'clock who?

Eight o'clock for dinner—now Peter's stomach hurts and he'll never know what time it is!

Would you say Peter's a modern guy?

No, he's always a little behind the times.

How about Doc Ock?
He's current!

**Which edition of the Daily Bugle
did Peter work for?**
The late edition.

What paper could Peter never work for?
The Times.

**What did Peter tell Jameson
when he missed his deadline?**

He gave him his *latest* excuse.

**What do you call it when Spider-Man falls
at the last second?**

A late slip.

CRIME DOESN'T PAY

What did Spider-Man say to the criminals he tied to a lamppost?

"Lighten up!"

How did the criminals feel when the cops cut them loose from the lamppost?
De-lighted.

Why did Peter run into the burning building?
He was all fired up to save people.

What did Doc Ock drive to the bank?
An *armored* car.

What did Doc Ock do at the bank?
He committed *armed* robbery.

Why did Peter push Aunt May out of the line of fire during the robbery?
Because they were in a savings bank.

What did Spider-Man do for the people at the bank?
He kept them out of *arm*'s way.

Why did Doc Ock destroy the train's controls?
He had a loco-motive.

Why was Spider-Man able to stop the last car from going off the tracks?
He'd *train*ed for these situations.

What would Spider-Man be if he had fallen onto the train tracks?
Hero-ick.

How was Spider-Man's time on the pier with Doc Ock?

Magnetic.

PICTURE THIS!

Why did Peter take so many pictures of M. J.?
He wanted to see what would develop with her.

When she was mad at him, what were M. J.'s thoughts about Peter's photos?
They were all negative.

How did M. J. look in the photos Peter took of her?
Picture perfect.

What would you call it if Peter didn't take any more pictures?
A photo finish.

What would Spider-Man use to take pictures?

A web-cam.

What kind of paper is the Bugle?

Note-able.

What section of the Bugle had news about John?

The orbit-uaries.

What kind of guy is the chief of the Daily Bugle?

One that toots his own horn.

INCR-EDIBLE!

What is Dr. Octavius's favorite snack food?

Inhibitor chips.

What happened to the pretzels when the convertible hit the cart?
They were a-salted.

How did things look to Peter when the pretzel cart flew over his head?
Twisted.

What did Peter say when he saw pretzels flying past him?
"There goes more dough slipping through my fingers!"

What did Dr. Octavius give Peter for lunch?
Food for thought.

What spice does Peter never have enough of?
Thyme.

TOTALLY BUGGIN'

What kind of dance does Spider-Man do?
The jitter-bug.

What kind of photographer is Peter?
A shutter-bug.

What paper does Peter work for?
The *Daily Bug-le*.

What does Spider-Man say when he's annoyed?
"Don't bug me."

What did Spider-Man read to get the news?
Fly paper.

What kind of advice does Spider-Man give?
Home-spun.

What do you get when you cross the young Mr. Osborn with Peter Parker?
A Harry spider.

What would you call Peter if he watched Jameson without him knowing?
A spy, duh!

How did Harry feel about Spider-Man?

Harry thought he was creepy.

What's the most unusual thing about Spider-Man?

He was raised by an aunt.

OH-PUN SEASON

How would you describe John's career?

He had a meteoric rise.

What kind of shoes did Miss Watson buy?

Mary Janes.

Harry: Peter, what can you tell me about the theory of relativity?

Peter: Well, there's my Aunt May, my Uncle Ben, and . . .

How did Peter feel about almost failing his class?

Physic-ally ill!

Why did Peter study atoms?

He knew how it felt to be split in two.

What do you call a talk Dr. Octavius gives at work?
A lab-oratory.

What kind of car does Dr. Octavius drive?
An Otto-mobile.

Why does Dr. Octavius believe in poetry?
He knows things could always
be verse.

What game would Doc Ock be good at?
Eight ball.

**Was Spider-Man good at catching
criminals?**
He was well suited for it.

Was May Parker nervous about her mortgage payments?
Yes, they made her aunt-sy.

What do you call someone who reads this book over and over?
A Spider-Maniac.